FOREVER
AMBER BROWN

Paula Danziger

FOREVER AMBER BROWN

Illustrated by Tony Ross

G. P. PUTNAM'S SONS   NEW YORK

*Special acknowledgment to Scott Hirschfeld and
his students at P.S. 87 New York City.*

Snap Snots is available from Forum Novelties, Oceanside, NY.

Text copyright © 1996 by Paula Danziger
Illustrations copyright © 1996 by Tony Ross
All rights reserved. This book, or parts thereof, may not be reproduced
in any form without permission in writing from the publisher.
G. P. Putnam's Sons, a division of The Putnam & Grosset Group,
200 Madison Avenue, New York, NY 10016.
G. P. Putnam's Sons, Reg. U.S. Pat. & Tm. Off.
Published simultaneously in Canada
Printed in the United States of America
Book design by Donna Mark
Lettering by David Gatti. Text set in Bembo

Library of Congress Cataloging-in-Publication Data
Danziger, Paula, 1944–   Forever Amber Brown / written by Paula Danziger;
illustrated by Tony Ross.   p.   cm.   Summary: Amber's life has
changed dramatically: her parents are divorced, her father lives
in France, her best friend has moved to another state,
and now her mother must decide whether to remarry.
[1. Family life—Fiction. 2. Remarriage—Fiction. 3. Friendship—Fiction.
4. Schools—Fiction.] I. Ross, Tony, ill. II. Title.
PZ7.D2394Fo   1996   [Fic]—dc20   96-19343   CIP   AC
ISBN 0-399-22932-9
1   3   5   7   9   10   8   6   4   2
First Impression

To all my readers, with love

FOREVER
AMBER BROWN

Chapter
One

I, Amber Brown, am on a search, not for gold, not for silver, not for treasure.

I, Amber Brown, am on a search for the perfect bowling ball. One that will help me beat my mom and Max, her friend.

I search.

Some holes are too far apart. Some are too close. Some balls weigh a ton. Some are an ugly color.

It is not an easy search, especially since my hair keeps falling in front of my eyes.

It's not easy to give up wearing two

ponytails and try to let my hair grow to be the same length.

I blow up at my hair. It goes up, and then falls down in front of my eyes again.

Finally, I find a bowling ball. My fingers don't get caught. It's not too heavy. It matches what I'm wearing.

I just wish that they made glitter bowling balls.

I rush back to our lane and begin.

I aim the ball down the middle, but it goes into the gutter.

Personally, I think that there's a magnet in my bowling ball, and one in each gutter.

"Better luck next time," Max says.

I sit down on the bench and sigh.

My mother picks up her bowling ball, aims, and throws.

There's no magnet in her ball.

It goes right down the center and hits the pin in the middle.

The bowling pins on each side are left standing.

"Split," Max says.

"Are you offering us a banana split?" I ask.

He crosses his eyes at me.

I know what a split is . . . that's what my mother has just gotten. . . . pins separated, with a hole in between them.

Max has also taught me other bowling words:

Strike—when all the pins go down with the first ball

I want to know why I, Amber Brown, get strikes only in baseball . . . not in bowling.

Spare—when you get all ten pins down with two balls

Turkey—three strikes in a row

I want to know why I, Amber Brown, bowl three times in a row, get low scores, and feel like a real turkey.

300—a perfect score

I, Amber Brown, got a 42 in our first game—an imperfect score.

Max bowls.

He gets a strike.

When he sits down on the bench, my mother gives him a kiss.

I think that's why he's been getting so many strikes, so that he gets kisses from my mother.

It's weird for me to see my mother kiss Max. I know she's divorced. I know that she and Max are going out . . . but it's still a little strange to see my mother and Max kissing.

I look away from them and watch the people in the next lane.

The little girl in that lane has forgotten to take her fingers out of the ball and she's now lying on the floor, crying, with the ball still on her hand.

When it's my turn, Max joins me on the lane and shows me, again, how to hold the ball, how to "approach," and how to throw.

This time my bowling ball doesn't bounce down the lane. . . . and six pins fall.

Max and I give each other high fives.

I get one more pin on my second ball, which touches the pin just before it drops into the gutter.

My mother gets four pins down.

Max only gets a spare next time he's up.

My mother gives him a kiss anyway because she says she has kisses to spare.

I don't remember my parents kissing each other very much at the end of the time they were married.

I actually like Max. I tried not to, but I do.

It's very confusing.

Half the time, I'm really glad that Max is in our lives, and the other half, I keep hoping that my mom and dad will get back together again.

The chance of my parents getting back together again is about as likely as my bowling a 300.

Part of me keeps hoping, though.

While I wait for my turn to bowl again, I look at people and try to guess their shoe sizes.

Then I look at the backs of their shoes, and if they're wearing rentals, I can see what sizes the shoes are.

I, Amber Brown, have no trouble making up games.

Some of the people have their own shoes, so there are no numbers on the backs.

Next, I start to think about what kinds of bowling shoes some of my favorite book characters would wear.

Dorothy, in *The Wizard of Oz*, would definitely wear red glitter bowling shoes.

I think about my favorite character when I was little, the Little Engine That Could. I wonder if engines wear shoes. Maybe if they're little, they wear training shoes.

My aunt Pam told me that in England, they call sneakers "trainers," so maybe that's what he would wear.

"Amber, it's your turn," my mother reminds me.

Gutter balls again.

"It's only a game," Max says.

When Max says that, I think of my father.

When I was little and my dad and I used

to play Chutes and Ladders and I'd lose and get upset, that's what he used to say: "It's only a game."

I used to wonder why he wouldn't just let me win if it was only a game.

My father . . . . . . I hardly ever see him now that he's living in Paris, France.

We talk every week, but that's not the same as seeing him.

I'm not even sure that I can see him in my brain anymore. I have to look at pictures of my dad to remember what he looks like.

I saw him during summer vacation, when my aunt Pam took me to London. My dad came to visit.

That was in August.

In September, I met Max.

Now it's October, and it's kind of weird.

I feel like I'm beginning to know Max better than my own father.

Next time my father calls, I'm going to beg him to move back.

Chapter
Two

Mrs. Holt says the words that I hate the most.

It's not: "Close your books now for a surprise quiz."

It's not: "Amber Brown, you're not doing your work, and I'm going to have to send a note home to your mother."

It's not: "You've got detention again for giggling and talking."

It's not: "Today, the cafeteria lunch is tuna-bacon burritos."

The dreaded words are: "Your school pictures are here."

I never used to care, not when I was a little kid. Now that I'm in the fourth grade, though, there are actually some people who I want to give my picture to, and I don't want them to barf when they see the picture.

I cross my fingers in my mind.

Please, oh, please, I think . . . . . . *make them look nice enough so that I can send one to Dad.*

I know that no matter what, he'll say that I look beautiful in the picture, because he always says that.

The day before I had my picture taken in kindergarten, I fell off the slide. I had a black eye, a bruised cheek, and cut marks on my nose. When my father saw those pictures, he said that the black, blue, and red made me look even more beautiful because now I had "not only a colorful personality, but a face to match." It was hard to believe him after that, but even my mom said, "You've got to love him for trying."

11

My parents don't love each other anymore, but they still love me, so that's two pictures that I'm going to need to order for sure.

"Hannah." Mrs. Holt hands Hannah Burton her pictures.

I hope that the camera took a picture of what Hannah is like inside—frog barf.

Probably not, since Hannah looks at them and says, "Lovely, as usual."

But then maybe Hannah Burton thinks that frog barf looks lovely.

Jimmy Russell and Bobby Clifford look at each other's pictures and make retching sounds.

They are such goofballs.

Then they look at Hannah Burton's picture and make more retching sounds.

Sometimes they aren't such goofballs.

I make a list in my brain of all the people who will get my picture if I end up looking human.

Justin Daniels, my old best friend, who moved to Alabama.

Brandi, my new best friend.

My grandparents—Mom's mom and my dad's parents—and my parents.

"Amber." Mrs. Holt smiles and hands me the envelope.

I take out my pictures and close my eyes.

Then I open my eyes.

The pictures look like me.

Brown hair.

Brown eyes.

My hair is slightly messy.

I don't understand it.

On the day the pictures were taken, Brandi came over to my house and we got ready for our pictures. She even helped me get my hair neat, and then when we got to school, she checked it just before the pictures were taken.

My hair still looks messy.

My nose still looks freckled even though I "borrowed" some of my mom's face makeup to cover the freckles.

"Let me see," Brandi says, handing me her pictures and looking at mine.

She looks terrific in her pictures.

"You look great," she says.

"Thank you." Hannah Burton holds up her pictures. "So nice of you to notice. I can't believe you'd be saying that about Amber."

I look at Hannah and smile. "Look, the order blank says that we can buy pictures, picture stickers, picture key chains, cups and plates with our pictures on them. Perhaps

15

after they see your pictures, they'll have picture toilet paper, too."

Just as Hannah starts to say something back, Marc Manchester yells, "I don't believe it. Look at the class picture."

I look at the class picture.

First I check to make sure that there's nothing wrong with me in the picture.

Marc says, "Fredrich Allen forgot to zip."

Everyone starts to laugh.

I feel sorry for Fredrich.

Actually, before the picture was taken, I whispered to him to remember not to pick his nose.

Actually, this is the first class picture where he isn't picking it.

I never thought to tell him to zip because somehow it's not something I usually check. Anyway, it would have been too embarrassing.

Mrs. Holt says, "That's enough. I wanted to retake the class picture anyway. I noticed that I forgot to put on my lipstick and mascara."

I look at the picture and smile at Mrs. Holt.

It's nice of her to try to have the class look at something other than Fredrich's zipper.

It doesn't work, though.

Jimmy Russell starts singing "Zip-A-Dee-Do-Da."

I look back at the order form and see that twelve pictures is the minimum order. I wonder what to do with the extra pictures.

Then I think of one more person to give one to . . . . . Max.

Then I wonder if I should.

What if my dad found out that I gave Max a picture? Would he get mad . . . or sad?

What if that gives Max ideas that he's like a part of the family?

If a picture is worth a thousand words, I, Amber Brown, want to be sure of what it's saying.

Chapter Three

"Knock, knock." My mother raps on my door and uses a tone of voice that lets me know that she's going to tell a dumb joke.

Ever since she started going out with Max, she's been telling silly jokes.

She used to be much more serious when she was married to my dad, but after the divorce she started to joke around more, and now sometimes, she's very silly. . . . even kind of embarrassing.

"Knock, knock," she calls out again.

I decide to play along with it. "Who's there?"

She opens the door and walks in. "Interrupting mother."

I grin at her and start to ask, "Interrupting mother who?" but just as I get the word "mother" out of my mouth, she interrupts me. "Clean up your room. It looks like a cyclone hit it."

I get the joke. . . . Interrupting mother interrupts. Yuk, yuk.

I also know that she's serious about my cleaning my room.

If she's so concerned about neatness, she should have given birth to a vacuum cleaner.

She continues with the knock-knock jokes. "Knock, knock."

"Who's there?"

"Interrupting cow."

I say, "Interrupt—" and she butts in and goes "Moo."

She can't seem to stop.

Interrupting vegetarian says, "Do you

know what the ingredients are in that hot dog?"

For interrupting giraffe, she just raises her neck way up.

There's only one way to stop her . . . by interrupting her jokes with a question. "Mom, on Monday, I have to bring in the order form for the pictures. Do you think we should buy any?"

She nods. "All of them. You know, you're beginning to look so grown-up."

"That's because I'm not wearing those dumb ponytails anymore," I inform her.

She pouts. "I love it when you wear those cute little ponytails."

"Mom, I'm not a little kid anymore, and I'm not a pony." I shake my head.

She leans over and picks up my hair so that I now have two ponytails.

"My cute little Amber," she says. "Now just remember, I don't want you to grow up too fast."

She starts moving the ponytails, one up and one down.

I feel like a human seesaw.

"Mom." I grin at her. "If you don't want me to grow up too fast, why are you always telling me not to be such a baby, to be more mature?"

"I don't say that much. . . . do I?" She

starts tickling my nose with one of the ponytails.

"Stop." My nose is beginning to tickle.

She continues.

I sneeze.

The sneeze lands on my hair and on her.

"You can't say that I didn't try to warn you." I sniff.

Letting go of my hair, she stands up. "I was just getting ready to take a shower anyway. Max and I are going out."

"Who's the Amber-sitter going to be?" I refuse to call the person who comes over to watch me a baby-sitter.

"Brenda."

I am so happy. Brenda is my favorite Amber-sitter. We always have such a good time, except for one thing. "Mom, can we send out for pizza? You're not going to ask Brenda to cook, are you?"

She shakes her head. "No, I tasted leftovers from the last time she cooked."

I remember that meal.

Brenda made meat loaf with a hard-boiled egg in it. She said her grandmother used to make it for her and it was one of her favorite meals growing up. I bet that her grandmother peeled the egg first.

"Pizza," my mother and I say at the same time.

I have some other questions that I want answered: "What time will you be home? Are you going to bring back a doggie-bag for me, filled with cheesecake? Is Max going to come into the house for a while?"

My mother starts to grin, gets up, and heads for the door.

After she goes out the door, she turns around and says, "Knock, knock."

"Who's there?" I can't believe that she's going to do another joke instead of answering my questions.

"Orange."

"Orange who?" I grin.

"Orange you glad this isn't another dumb interrupting joke?"

Then she laughs and leaves.

I can't believe her!

She's always telling me to act my age . . . . and then she doesn't act her age.

I wonder if other parents are ever like that.

Chapter
Four

The doorbell rings.

It's Max.

He's got two bunches of flowers.

One of them is for my mother—red roses.

The other one is for me—purple flowers.

These are the first flowers that anyone has ever given me.

Once, when Justin was six, he gave me some flowers, but they were stinkweeds.

Somehow I don't think that this is the same, since when Justin gave them to me, he said, "Stinkweeds for a stinker," and when

Max gave us the flowers, he said, "For two of the most important people in my life."

If my dad lived closer, I'm sure that *he* would bring flowers.

We go into the kitchen so that Mom can get vases for the flowers.

The doorbell rings again.

This time it's Brenda.

Her hair is a different color, sort of a weird pink, and she's carrying a small piece of luggage.

Her hair is always changing color.

We give each other a big hug.

If I had an older sister, I would want it to be Brenda.

When my school pictures arrive, I'm going to give her one.

We go into the kitchen.

My mom and Max are kissing each other.

I really wish they would stop doing that.

"Ahem." Brenda clears her throat.

Max and Mom move away from each other, just a little.

My mother blushes.

Brenda goes over and gives Mom a hug. "Hi, Sarah."

Brenda used to call my mother Mrs. Brown. Then, when my mom changed her name back to Thompson, Mom decided that Brenda should just call her Sarah.

Brenda smiles at Max. "Hi, Max."

My mother grins. "Hi. Nice hair color. And what's with the suitcase? Are you planning on spending the night? Running away from home?"

Brenda grins back. "Tonight I thought that Amber and I could play beauty salon after she works on her book report . . . if that's okay with you, Sarah."

My mother looks at Brenda, then at me, then at Max, then back at Brenda. "You're not planning to change my daughter's hair color, are you?"

"Can she pierce my ears?" I've been begging to get my ears pierced forever, but I have to wait three whole years, until I'm twelve. Twelve . . . . . . by that time I could be someone else's baby-sitter.

"Don't worry." Brenda opens up the suitcase to show her. "We'll be putting on a

face mask, playing with some makeup, trying out different hairstyles, painting our
nails."

"Sounds like fun," my mother says, then
looks at Max and teases, "Maybe I should
stay here and play beauty salon, too."

He shakes his head. "You're beautiful just
the way you are. We, my dear, are going
out. I have plans for us."

Sometimes Max sounds so soppy, so
goopy—just like one of those nighttime television shows.

My mother doesn't seem to mind.

After they leave, Brenda says, "They look
so cute together."

I'm not sure that I want my mother and
Max to look so cute together.

The doorbell rings.

Pizza.

And then we raid the freezer.

Four flavors of ice cream . . . just little
scoops . . .

"Next time," Brenda says, "I'll make you my latest recipe—Velveeta whipped potatoes and spaghetti diablo."

Sometimes Brenda reminds me of Indian beaded jewelry . . . the way one bead can break the pattern and then the jewelry is not perfect. It's like Brenda's cooking is the thing that keeps her from being the perfect Amber-sitter.

"Let's beauty salon now." I can't even think about her latest recipe.

"First, your homework." She clears the table. "Brains are as important as beauty."

An almost perfect Amber-sitter . . . if it weren't for her cooking and her memory of my homework assignments.

She grins at me. "You don't have to start your report now . . . . . ."

I grin back.

She finishes the sentence: ". . . if you let me make the spaghetti diablo for you right now."

Language arts homework, here I come.

Chapter Five

Book Report
Using a book, or books, that you
have read this marking period, make
up a game that will be fun to play.

I, Amber Brown, wouldn't mind homework so much if it weren't so much work
and if I didn't have to do so much of it at
home.

I, Amber Brown, actually like the book
reports that we do in class. I like them after
they are all done and we share them with
each other.

It's just all the time it takes to do the work . . . . at home.

My author cards are already finished . . . . . ten authors, four books each.

My game is like go fish and authors, only I call it "build your own library."

Bruce Coville
Planet of the Dips

Judy Blume
Superfudge

Build Your Own Library

Walter Dean Myers.
Hoops

You ask for an author whose card you have in your hand, and then if the other player has any of that author's book cards, you get it or them. When you have all four, it becomes a "boxed set," and you get to put it into your library. The person with the most books in his or her library wins.

I write real fancy letters, *BUILD YOUR OWN LIBRARY,* all over the gift box that my aunt Pam used to send me a new sweater. Then I put stickers all over the box.

Inside the box, I put the directions sheet, which explains how to play and tells something about each of the authors that I have chosen . . . . . Avi, Judy Blume, Daniel Pinkwater, Bruce Coville, Walter Dean Myers, Margaret Mahy, Lois Lowry, Beverly Cleary, Robert Kimmel Smith, and Gary Paulsen.

I, Amber Brown, have read every book that is on the cards. I love to read.

Now that the book report is done, I

am happy and proud that I did it. I hope that Mrs. Holt likes it. I hope that she doesn't assign another report for a while. Fat chance! Mrs. Holt's first name is Roberta . . . . . I think it should be Reporta.

Brenda looks at the cards. "Amber, you did a great job. I think that these cards are going to get worn down and messed up pretty quickly if you don't do something about it. Look, I can ask my father to laminate the cards at his office."

"Will he do that?" I hope so.

Brenda nods her pink head and then laughs. "Sure. Actually, he'll ask his secretary to do it. When they first got the machine, he tried to do it but got his tie caught in the laminator."

I giggle.

So does Brenda. Then she mimes trying to get him unattached from the laminator.

Brenda really is so fun.

Until she started to Amber-sit, it used to

be so boring. . . . Now I have a great time.

I'm going to miss her when she goes to college next year. She wants to be a teacher or a librarian . . . . or a television stylist.

I finish up, and beauty salon begins.

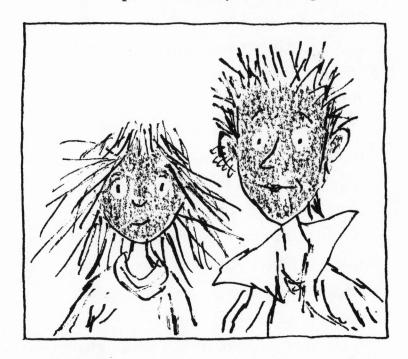

Brenda mixes some water with some stuff from a box and smears the mixture on our faces.

It's so weird.

At first, it feels like wet clay, like I'm in the middle of a Silly Putty box . . . . . and then it starts to dry.

"Don't move your face." Brenda sounds a little like a robot. "Or it will crack."

No moving, no smiling, no frowning . . . . . I, Amber Brown, sit absolutely still. I, Amber Brown, have trouble sitting absolutely still.

I wonder if this is what the presidents on Mt. Rushmore feel like.

My nose starts to itch.

I've got to sneeze.

Concentrating on not sneezing, I look around my bedroom and try to concentrate on something else.

My room looks so baby.

I, Amber Brown, need a more grown-up room.

After all, on my next birthday I will be a double-digit kid . . . . . the big ten. Even though that won't be for a while, I should get a more grown-up room.

The room hasn't been decorated since I was six. Three of the walls are yellow. I used to like that color yellow . . . now it looks like the little river of "water" that Brandi's new puppy leaves on the floor.

The fourth wall has dancing ballerina wallpaper. And they aren't even human dancing ballerinas. They're hippos and ducks and elephants and rhinos and rabbits.

I, Amber Brown, am a nine-year-old trapped in a six-year-old's room . . . . . and it's time for some changes.

Chapter
Six

Cheerios. Milk. Bananas.

I am eating my second-favorite breakfast and waiting for my mother to wake up so that I can convince her to let me redecorate my room.

My first-favorite breakfast is English muffins with lots of peanut butter on both pieces . . . and M&M happy faces on the peanut butter.

That is not my mother's idea of a "healthy breakfast," though . . . so I don't get to eat it at our house.

When my dad still lived in New Jersey,

right after he and Mom separated, he let me eat my favorite breakfast at his apartment. Once, he even made one for me and one for him. But he made his with an unhappy face because by that time, he knew that his company was sending him to Paris, France.

I look at the Cheerios and think of Justin. Once, when we were little, we had a contest to see who could stick the most Cheerios up our noses. Justin won because he also poured some milk in and made stuff mushier.

Needless to say, our parents were not very happy with us.

I wonder if, right now, in Alabama, Justin

is eating Cheerios and milk and bananas
. . . or sticking them up his nose. I wonder
if he still remembers that we did that.

Maybe he's eating some weird Southern
food like grits and hush puppies. He once
wrote and told me that he's eating that stuff
now. It kind of sounds like now that he's
moved, he's eating dirt and has turned into
an animal cannibal.

My mother walks into the kitchen, yawn-
ing.

Before she even has time to get a cup of
coffee, I jump up and say, "Mom, I NEED
to have my room decorated. It's just so
baby. And you got yours redone after Dad

left . . . so now it's my turn."

My mother lowers one eyelid and says, "Amber."

I can't stop myself. "You're always saying that I should take better care of my room . . . well, if I'm proud of it, I'll take better care of it."

"Amber." My mother closes both eyes for a second, then opens them wide and points to the chair that I've just left. "Sit."

What does she think I am, a trained dog?

She's got a look on her face that makes me sit.

"Arf, arf," I say, trying to make her laugh.

She pours a cup of coffee.

I hold up the papers that I worked on last night, the chart and lists that explain why I should have my room redone. "Please," I say. "Just look at these papers. I worked sooooooooo hard on them. After you look, I just know that you'll say yes."

Actually, I'm beginning to think that maybe I'm not handling this the way I should . . . that maybe I should have let her wake up first and maybe asked her about her date with Max.

But I've already started and I can't seem to stop . . . kind of like the time the brakes on my bike stopped working and I ended up hitting a tree.

My mother is beginning to look like that tree.

She sits down next to me and looks at the papers.

She starts to frown . . . then she smiles at something.

Maybe I have a chance.

Then she frowns again.

She is definitely not being a happy-face mother this morning.

She sighs.

Then she sighs again.

Then she speaks. "Amber, some of these are very good reasons for redoing your room. Some are not. In fact, some are pretty annoying."

"Please. Ignore the ones that don't work. Just look at the ones that you agree with." I place my hands together so that it looks like a combination of begging and praying. "Oh, please. Oh, pretty please. Oh, pretty please with sugar on top."

My mother starts to smile.

I stick my face right in front of hers. "Pu-leeze."

She moves back a little. "Amber Brown, I just don't know what I'm going to do with you."

"I do." I grin. "You're going to say, 'Yes,

my darling daughter, I will help you redecorate your room. I realize that you're growing up and need the change.' "

My mother shakes her head, a little sadly. "No, honey. There are several reasons why we can't do it right now. One is that I'm a little short of money at this time."

"I'll give up my allowance for six months," I offer. "And I've got a little bit of money saved up. We can use that, too."

My mother puts her hand on my arm. "There's another reason, honey."

I look at her.

She continues. "I don't know how much longer we're going to be living here."

I feel like someone has thrown a medicine ball at my chest. "Why?"

She tells me. "Last night Max asked me to marry him, and while I'm not sure of my answer, I do know that it's not a good idea to make any long-term plans involving the house."

I don't say anything for a minute, and
then I ask, "What about Daddy? I always
thought that when he came back to America, the two of you would try again."

She shakes her head.

I say, "So why can't things stay the way
they are . . . you and me together . . . you
going out with Max . . . but not getting
married?"

She sighs.

"It's too soon," I say. "You've only been going out since the summer. It's only October."

"I know," she says. "I said that to him already. But you know, Amber, he really loves me a lot. And I love him, too. And he loves you."

I was beginning to like Max . . . a lot. But love . . . that's Big Time.

My mother takes a sip of coffee. "I've got to do some serious thinking about this . . . so I'm sorry, but your room is not going to be redecorated right now."

My room . . . I forgot all about it.

One minute, I want to get one thing in my life changed, and the next minute, I find out that my whole entire life might change.

I, Amber Brown, will never complain again about stupid dancing animal wallpaper.

In fact, now I want things to stay exactly as they are.

Chapter
Seven

"Bulletin, bulletin, bulletin." Brandi sits down next to me in Elementary Extension.

Having to stay after school until your mother picks you up after work isn't so bad when your best friend also has to stay after until her mother picks her up.

I, Amber Brown, have two best friends . . . one here, Brandi . . . . and Justin, who is in Alabama.

I don't like one better. I just like them differently.

"Bulletin, bulletin, bulletin," Brandi repeats. "Major breaking story."

"How did the story break? Did you drop it?" I tease.

"Bulletin, bulletin, bulletin." Ever since Brandi decided that she wants to be a newscaster when she grows up, she's been saying, "Bulletin, bulletin, bulletin," for everything.

Ten minutes ago, she said it when she reported that the janitor had just changed a fluorescent light bulb. So I don't take her announcements very seriously.

She sees something and then she immediately reports it as if it's the most important thing in the entire world.

You could say that she's faster than a speeding bullet-in.

"This one is major . . . . major . . . major." She grins at me.

Ms. Smith, the Elementary Extension teacher, walks in and sits down at her desk.

"Major," Brandi whispers.

"What is it?" I ask.

"Take out your homework and start on it now, quietly," Ms. Smith says. "It's been a long, difficult day, and I have a headache."

I, Amber Brown, am sorry that she's got a headache . . . . but it's not fair that everyone in the entire after-school program has to be quiet.

It's not as if it's detention or anything . . . . we just have to stay there until someone picks us up . . . so that we're not latchkey kids, who go home with no grown-ups around until they come home from work.

I take out my book and pretend to work.

So does Brandi.

Oh yes, we're the great pretenders.

"So?" I whisper. "Tell me."

"I overheard the principal talking to the sixth-grade teacher. And guess what? There are going to be a whole bunch of new kids coming into the school. You know the land that used to be a farm at the edge of town . . . where all those new houses are being built? Well, that means that there will probably be a lot of new kids coming into the school. Maybe some of them will be fourth-graders. Won't that be fun?"

Fun?!

Ha. I don't think so.

We have a really small class, and I used to think it would be fun to get some new, different kids, maybe have Hannah Burton move to the moon . . . . but right now I want things to stay the same . . . . here at school, at least.

"Quiet. I mean it," Ms. Smith says.

Brandi and I play a connect-the-dot game.

I win five times.

She wins twice.

I think she's too excited thinking about her news to concentrate on the game.

I think I'd rather concentrate on the game than on thinking about her news.

My mother walks into the classroom and says hello to Ms. Smith.

I jump up.

My knees hit the bottom of the desktop.

I think that someone should invent foam-rubber backings to put on the bottoms of desktops.

Ms. Smith is so sweet to my mother.

It makes me want to puke.

We walk out to the car.

My mother says, "Amber, honey."

"Amber, honey" at the very beginning of a conversation usually means that there's big news, not always news that I want to hear.

That's my mother's way.

"I have something important to tell you."

Bulletin, bulletin, bulletin, I think. She's going to tell me that she's decided to marry Max and we're going to have to move.

My legs feel like they've lost their knees.

We get to the car.

There are two suitcases in the backseat.

"Amber," she says, "I need to take a few days to think and work some things out. We're going to Alabama . . . . to see the Danielses."

Justin.

I'm going to see Justin.

Chapter Eight

Life is very strange sometimes.

One minute, I'm in Elementary Extension, waiting for my mother to pick me up and take me home . . . . home to dinner . . . . . home to homework, and the next minute, I'm on a plane on my way to Alabama, where I'm going to see my old best friend, Justin Daniels.

Actually, it's not the next minute. It's a couple of hours. From the school, to the airport, to the terminal, and then we ran, RAN, to get on the plane. It was like we

were in training for a new Olympic event, the Airplane Decathalon.

We're up in the air right now. Actually, I'm beginning to wonder if my mother is becoming permanently up in the air.

I can't believe that the woman sitting next to me is my very own mother. My real mother never lets me stay out of school unless I'm practically dying. My real mother never misses work unless she's practically dying. And tomorrow is Friday and we're not going to school or work and we're both perfectly healthy. The mother I know never goes on trips without planning them for a long time. At breakfast, neither of us knew this was going to happen.

I look at the woman sitting next to me.

She looks like my mother.

She smells like my mother. Her perfume is the same.

She sounds like my mother.

I wonder if all mothers get this weird when someone asks them to marry him.

I wonder if all mothers would call their best friends the way that my mom called Justin's mother this morning, and if they would just rush home, quickly pack suitcases, and take off to talk.

My mother is definitely not the mother I've always known.

My mother is sitting next to me, making lists of why she should marry Max and why she shouldn't marry Max.

I ask her if I can see the lists, but she says no.

I start making my own lists.

One is the reasons why my mother should marry Max. One is the reasons why she shouldn't.

I let her see what I'm doing.

"Amber, honey, when you're done, I'd like to see your lists." She hands me her packet of peanuts.

I, Amber Brown, will not take bribes. I will, however, take the peanuts. "I will show you my lists if you show me your lists."

She shakes her head. "It's just too private."

She may think it's "too private," but

what she's going to decide is going to be very important to my life.

I pretend to be looking around the plane and sneak looks at her lists when I can.

She puts her hand over the lists, just like kids in school do when they don't want the kid next to them to cheat off their papers.

She looks over at my papers. I put my hand over my lists.

I work on my lists.

Reasons for My Mother to Marry Max:

1. He's nice to her.

2. He's nice to me.

3. He's funny.

4. He's teaching me to bowl.

5. They love each other.

6. He says he loves me.

Reasons for My Mother Not to Marry Max:

1. What if my father comes back and wants to marry my mother again?

2. There's not enough room in our house.

3. He doesn't always remember to put the toilet seat down. What if they're married and he uses the bathroom and forgets to put the toilet seat down? What if I go to the bath-room late at night, and the toilet seat is up, and I don't notice it and sit down and fall into the water?

4. If he's living in the house, there will be no real privacy. I won't be able to walk around in my nightgown.

5. If he's living in the house, he'll be sleeping in my mother's bedroom. I don't think I'm going to like that. I

won't be able to just go in and talk
to her whenever I want.

Nothing in my life is staying the same,
except for my room.

It will be so good to see Justin and his
family again . . . all of us together. I just hope
that it'll be just the way it was when he lived
on my street, before we found out that he
was going to have to move away.

The flight attendant makes an announce-
ment that we should put on our seat belts,
put up our trays, and place our chairs in the
upright position.

The little girl in the seat across from me
holds her Barbie doll in her lap and puts the
seat belt around both of them.

Her Barbie doll reminds me of Tiffani
Shroeder. She's got this little brother,
Howie, who is always doing weird things
with her collection of Barbies.

Today at school, Tiffani opened her

lunch. Now that she's decided to be a vegetarian, she eats a lot of salads. Howie rear-
ranged it so that it looked like a real *bed* of
lettuce. There was lettuce on the bottom,

and then Barbie. There was more lettuce on
top of Barbie, and a carrot "pillow" under
her head. He made it look like the blue
cheese dressing was coming out of the Barbie's mouth so that it was like puke.

It was one of Howie's best creations.

The plane makes a little bump as it lands.

"Don't worry," the little girl says to her Barbie. "There's nothing to be scared of."

That Barbie has a good life . . . someone saying that there's nothing to be scared of.

I bet that Barbie doll never had parents who got divorced.

I bet that the Ken doll never moves away.

I bet that she never has to worry about what grade she's going to get on her Barbie book report.

I, Amber Brown, who have never liked Barbie dolls, am now jealous of how easy their lives are.

Somehow everything always stays the same for them.

I wonder what an Amber Brown doll on a bed of lettuce would look like.

Maybe I should make one and send it to Max, with a note saying, "Lettuce Alone."

I hope that when Mom and Mrs. Daniels talk, my mother decides to let things stay the way they are.

I'm only nine years old.

It's enough that I have to change and grow up.

I think that grown-ups should have done all their growing up by the time they have children . . . so that children can make their changes while everything around them stays the same.

I really hope that Justin hasn't changed a lot.

I'm so excited.

In just a few minutes, I'm going to see him.

I can't wait.

Chapter Nine

Everyone's at the airport.

Well, not everyone in the world is at the airport, but the whole Daniels family is there.

I can see them waiting for us at the other end of the hall.

I am so excited.

I'm also a little shy.

It's been almost six months since they've moved away.

I keep walking toward them.

Justin's taller.

He's always been taller than I am, but now he's much taller.

How come everyone seems to be getting taller than me?

Other people have growth spurts.

I, Amber Brown, have growth dribbles.

Even Danny, his little brother, looks taller.

Mr. and Mrs. Daniels are still the same height . . . not the same height as each other . . . the same height they've always been . . . well not always . . . but since I've known them.

Mrs. Daniels has gained some weight, though.

She must be eating a lot of grits and hush puppies.

I start running toward them.

When I get there, I'm still feeling a little shy.

I, Amber Brown, don't know what to say.

Justin says nothing either.

We just look at each other.

I wiggle my ears, twitch my nose, and stick my tongue out at him.

He wiggles his ears, twitches his nose, and sticks his tongue out at me. Then he gives me a punch on the arm.

I give him a punch on the arm.

It's just like it always was.

Danny is jumping up and down. "Amber Brown is still a crayon."

I push his baseball cap down over his eyes. "Danny Daniels is still a pain."

He continues to jump up and down. "Danny Daniels is still a brain."

"P," I say, "not B-R. . . . P . . . pain."

"P," Danny says. "No. I don't have to . . . . I just went."

Four-year-olds always think that body stuff is so funny.

Danny keeps repeating "P, p, p," and jumping up and down like he's got to go to the bathroom.

My mother hugs Mrs. Daniels. "I'm so glad to see you."

"P, p, p." Danny can't stop laughing.

"He hasn't changed." I grin at Justin.

Justin shakes his head. "He hasn't changed the way he acts . . . . and sometimes

I think he hasn't changed his clothes either."

"Oh, stink." I hold my nose.

"Enough, you two. Don't start teasing Danny already. It's not fair . . . two against one." Mr. Daniels picks up my mom's and my suitcases.

"You two just wait until the new baby is born . . . then we can gang up on you."

New baby . . . new baby . . . . so that's why Mrs. Daniels looks like she's getting fat.

We all start walking through the terminal to the car.

Danny is hopping around, saying, "P, p, p."

"I hope that you're hungry," Mrs. Daniels says. "We've decided to take you to Say Cheese, the new restaurant in town. They have the best pizza."

"Pizza!" Justin and I yell at the same time. We both pretend to be holding something up with our fingers. "Hold the anchovies."

Then we both laugh so hard that it hurts.

Justin and I are doing some of the same things that we've always done.

It makes me so happy.

It makes me so happy that I almost forget the reason why we're here . . . so that my mom can decide whether or not to marry Max.

I almost forget . . . . but not quite.

Chapter
Ten

Say Cheese . . . . . I love it. It's my new
favorite restaurant in the world.

You can order all kinds of things with
cheese on them.

Pasta . . . . . pizza . . . . vegetables
. . . . . . burritos . . . cheesecake . . . . Cheez
Doodles . . . . dumplings . . . gazillions of
things made with cheese.

Justin and I order our favorite—pizza
with extra cheese.

I look at Justin.

It's so good to see him.

He looks almost the same, just a little different.

We all sit at the table, waiting for our order to arrive.

It's so good to see the Danielses.

It feels like a missing piece of me is back again . . . . like I'm an Amber jigsaw puzzle that had a piece missing from the middle . . . . not from an edge, where it doesn't really matter.

My mother and Mrs. Daniels are holding each other's hands.

Mr. Daniels is grinning while he pours sodas for everyone.

Danny is jumping up and down, begging for money to buy tokens.

I don't blame him.

I want tokens, too.

Say Cheese is incredible.

There are all of these machines . . . pinball, video games, virtual reality.

People can rent Polaroid cameras here, or buy the kind of camera that you use once and then throw away after the film is developed, or people can bring their own cameras.

We all eat our pizza and then rush around and have our pictures taken.

It's so much fun.

"Say cheese!" Mr. Daniels yells from the platform above us.

Justin and I look up.

We're lying down on a wooden circle painted to look like a pizza.

Justin is dressed up like a slice of pepperoni.

I'm a green pepper.

Danny jumps onto the "pie," pretends to take a bite out of Justin's leg, and yells, "I LOVE pepperoni pizza."

"Dead meat." Justin rolls over and starts tickling Danny.

I join in and tickle Danny under the armpits.

We have to quit when one of the Say Cheese people comes over. "Okay, you kids. Give someone else a chance."

We trade our pepperoni costumes with a king and queen. We keep changing costumes . . . . gladiators . . . . space aliens . . . . dragons . . . . and doctors with Danny as our not-so-patient patient.

Rushing back to the table, we take a soda break.

Then it's off to the machines.

Justin and I stand in front of my favorite game, "Whack-a-Mole."

There are a whole bunch of holes, and every once in a while a mole sticks its head out, and I try to hit it with a foam-rubber hammer-thingy. It's not easy to explain, but it sure is fun to do. And they're not real-live moles; they're plastic.

Somehow, hitting the moles on their heads reminds me of Tiffani Schroeder. "Justin, remember Tiffani? She's a vegetarian now . . . and she's joined a lot of groups that are against cruelty to animals."

Justin hits a mole on its head. "Are there any groups that are *for* cruelty to animals? I bet there aren't."

I giggle. "The Whack-a-Mole Society. WAMS."

As Justin hits another mole, he yells, "WAMS!"

I continue to talk. "Tiffani says that she won't eat any animals that have parents."

"In science class, we learned that some animals eat their young," Justin says.

"Yug," I say.

He hands the mallet to me. "I tried to convince my parents that it would be all right to eat Danny . . . . but they said no."

"Tiffani also says that she won't eat any animals with eyes," I continue.

"I bet that she doesn't eat corn, either." Justin laughs.

"Corn's not an animal. It's a vegetable, goofball," I remind him.

"Yeah . . . . . but if she won't eat anything with eyes, she probably won't eat anything with ears . . . . ears of corn, get it?"

I groan.

We go back to the table for more soda and more tokens.

My mom and Mrs. Daniels are still talking seriously.

I wish I knew what they were talking about.

I, Amber Brown, want to know.

I, Amber Brown, need to know.

Chapter
Eleven

"You can open your eyes now," Justin says.

Sitting in the tree house in Justin's backyard, I open my eyes.

Justin is holding something in his hand that looks a lot like snot coming out of his nose.

He takes it out and hands it to me. "Cool, huh?"

"Yuk," I say. "Thanks . . . . . but no thanks."

He laughs and hands me a piece of cardboard with something covered with plastic.

It's called "Snap Snots."

The directions say:

It may be necessary to trim bow
before inserting into nostril.
Trim with scissors.
When gently STRETCHED &
RELEASED, *SNAP SNOTS* will
sail LONG distances. Wash with
soap & water when dusty.

"It's for you. A present. It's not real snot
. . . . but it looks good, huh? All of my
friends have it. We've started a club: the
Royal Order of the Snots . . . and I'm the
grand booger. That's kind of like presi-
dent."

"There are only boys in this club, right?"
I ask.

He nods. "How did you guess?"

I, Amber Brown, would never join that
club . . . . and I don't think that Brandi
would either . . . . but I bet most of the boys
in my class would join.

There are certain things I know: I
wouldn't join the Royal Order of the Snots
. . . I would never own a Barbie doll. I also
know that I will never have another friend
like Justin . . . and I know that I wish he still
lived near me.

I look at the Snap Snot, and then I look
at Justin. "Thanks. I'll keep it forever."

"Can I come up?" Danny yells.

Justin walks over to the tree house door, looks down at his little brother, and yells, "No."

"I'm going to tell." Danny starts to cry.

Times like this I know why I like being an only child.

I look down.

Danny is lying on the ground, kicking his feet.

Mr. Daniels comes up to him. "Danny, let's go to the store. We'll pick up some ice cream for dessert."

Danny keeps on yelling.

Justin looks down and yells, "Stop being such a baby. In a couple of months, you're going to be a middle child."

Danny starts to kick his feet even more.

"And I'm still going to be the big brother," Justin yells down.

Mr. Daniels shakes a finger at Justin. "I suggest that you act like the big brother, the

GOOD, KIND, UNDERSTANDING big brother. Now tell Danny that you're sorry."

Justin just stands for a minute, and then yells down, "I'm sorry. I'm sorry. I'm sorry."

"Much better," his father says, picking up Danny, whispering something in his ear, and heading to his car.

Justin looks down at them, and then comes back and sits next to me. "I'm sorry that he's such a pain. I'm sorry that he drives me nuts. I'm sorry that he's always following me all over the place. I bet that my dad's just bribed the little twerp. He does that a lot. Danny's gotten really weird since we found out about the new baby coming."

"Does it bother you?" I ask.

Justin shrugs. "Nah."

Justin doesn't like to let people know when stuff bugs him.

I learned that about him when he had to move away.

I've also learned that I can't ask him too much about how he feels or he backs off.

My mom says that's the way a lot of boys are and I'm just going to have to get used to it.

Justin slugs me on the arm. "Why don't you start a club back home? The Royal Order of the Snots . . . . you could be the grand booger of the East."

"I'll think about it." I can't really imagine that happening.

This reminds me of something. I know that it's something that he'd like to know. "Remember Brandi?"

Justin nods.

"Well, she's got this special trick she can do. She takes a wad of newly chewed gum out of her mouth, puts it around her nose, blows, and makes a bubble."

"Cool," Justin says.

I, Amber Brown, think about my two best friends and their weirdnesses. Both do kind of gross things having to do with their noses.

It makes me laugh to think that. . . . . Everyone "nose" that it's "snot" funny to be so gross.

I change the subject. "Justin . . . you know my mom is thinking of getting married to Max, who you've never met."

Justin nods. "Do you like him?"

"Yeah. I like him, but I don't know that I want him to live in my house."

"YOUR house?" Justin kids. "You live there alone?"

"Mine and Mom's. Justin . . . . this is serious."

"I know." He stops smiling.

"I want everything to go back to normal," I say, thinking of the way it was when my dad lived with us, when Justin and his family lived down the street.

"This *is* normal," Justin says. "It's weird.

Things change . . . . and then they become normal. I think that's what grown-ups already know and we have to learn."

"I don't want to learn it." I make a face.

"I didn't, either." Justin picks up the Snap Snot and puts it up his nose.

Then he looks at me. "But I had to . . . and it's not so bad. I'm having fun here now, and I have new friends . . . and you're still my friend."

I think about it. What's normal? Do things always change? Would they have changed even if my mom and dad stayed together? Would it be so terrible if Max was living with us . . . . . if he was my stepfather . . . . . STEPFATHER. . . . ? Would it be better if my mom said she didn't want to marry him? What if Max wasn't in our lives? What would it be like if my mom was dating other guys? What if . . . . . What if . . . . . What if???????????????????

Max . . . . Mom . . . . Dad . . . . . I'll think about it tomorrow.

It's all too much to think about right now. . . . I open my package of Snap Snots and put it in my nose.

Chapter Twelve

"So what did you decide?" I ask.

My mother is packing our bags.

It's Sunday morning and we're still at the Danielses' house and she still hasn't told me what she's going to say to Max.

"I still haven't decided." She sits down on her bed in the guest room.

I'm sitting on my bed. "Maybe you just shouldn't decide. Maybe you should just let things go on the way they are. Why is this so important right now? You've only been going out together for a couple of months."

She bites her lip. "Max has been offered a great job in California."

I gasp. "California? Would we have to move to California?"

It hits my brain all at once. Pow. We'd have to move . . . . and move far away. Pow. I'd have to leave my house . . . my friends

. . . my school . . . Pow. And what about
when Daddy moves back? He would still be
far away.

She shakes her head. "No. If I say yes and
Max and I get engaged, we'll stay in New
Jersey . . . at least for a while. It's just that
Max doesn't want to give up the job if
I'm not willing to make a commitment.
He loves me very much . . . and you, too
. . . . and he wants us to be a family. It's not
even that we have to get married right away.
He just wants us to be engaged . . . more
committed."

I pull at a thread on the bedspread. "Why
can't you decide?"

She sighs. "It's all so soon. Max was the
first man that I dated after the divorce.
When we first started going out, I thought
he would be just the beginning of my new
social life . . . and then we fell in love."

"You're in love with him?" I've never
heard her say that.

She smiles and nods.

"You're in love with him?" I repeat.

She nods again. "Does that bother you?"

I think about Max . . . . how nice he is, how much I like him. I think about how he helps me with my schoolwork, takes us places, is teaching me how to bowl. I think about how happy my mother is when she's with him.

"No. I guess not. I really like him a lot . . . . but it's kind of weird . . . to think about him as being part of our family." I pull some more on the thread and think for a moment about my dad.

My mother comes over, sits down, takes the thread out of my hand, and pushes it back into the bedspread. "Amber, I've just about made my decision."

"And . . . ." I want to know.

She nods. "I want to be engaged to Max . . . . and eventually marry him, but I know that this decision affects you . . . and I want to know how you feel about it. . . . Max wants to know, too. And he wants me to tell you how much he loves you and how hard he will try not to disrupt your life and how he wants all of us to be part of each other's lives."

"When did he tell you that?" I ask.

"When he asked me to marry him," she says.

"That was definitely a long proposal," I say, and smile.

She smiles back. "It was. We did a lot of talking . . . and Max says that if, when, I say yes, he wants to talk to you about every-thing. . . ."

"This is going to be a family where a lot of talking goes on." I grin.

Then I realize what I've just said: "This is going to be a family," and I realize that it IS going to be a family . . . and I, Amber Brown, feel good about it. I like the idea. I like the idea a lot.

We were a family when my parents were together. We were a family when my parents divorced . . . a different kind of family . . . and we're going to be a family when Max is part of it . . . another different family.

My mother repeats . . . "This is going to be a family. . . ."

We look at each other and know that the decision is made.

Now we just have to tell Max.

Now I just have to tell my father . . . because he's still a part of my family . . . . just not a part of this one that is going to be.

There's a knock on the door.

"Knock, knock." It's Justin.

My mother and I look at each other, smile, and say, "Who's there?"

"Interrupting Justin," he yells in.

I've told him all of the dumb interrupting jokes.

"Interrupting Jus—" my mother and I say at the same time.

He interrupts, "Just want to let you know that it's time to go back to Say Cheese. I'm hungry and we've got to watch the guy hold the anchovies."

I, Amber Brown, am beginning to realize that while some things change . . . some things stay the same.

I know that no matter what happens, one thing will be the same—no matter how many changes there are. I will always be Forever Amber Brown.